Sky Cloud City

Enjoy! :)

Maria Karouvalakis

The Adventures of Hope & Trusty

Sky Cloud City

Maria Kamoulakou-Marangoudakis

Illustrated by Aspasia Arvanitis

Illuminated caps illustrated by the author

First printing March 2016.

Publisher: Pierce Press / Gigglequick Books
10 Court St., #206
Arlington, MA 02476-0206
PiercePress.com and IPNE.org

Softcover ISBN: 978-0-9776396-8-7
Hardcover ISBN: 978-0-9776396-7-0

Library of Congress number pending
Fifty pages, 8-1/2 x 11" trim
Printed in the USA.
Distributed by Ingram, Pierce Press, and the Author.

Author: Maria Kamoulakou-Marangoudakis
Illustrator: Aspasia Arvanitis
Illustrated capital letters: Maria Kamoulakou-Marangoudakis
Editor: Tanya Gold
Book design and layout: Cate Rickard Barr
Cover design: Charlotte Pierce with Cate Rickard Barr
Maria Kamoulakou photograph by Mark Archer
Aspasia Arvanitis photograph by Edward J. Parent

Dedicated to my parents
Sophia and Theodoros,
who instilled in me
the love of ancient Greece.

Winner of the premiere Sky Cloud City illustration contest is 10-year-old Andreas from Crete, Greece.

Once upon a time, in a faraway land, across the deep blue sea, there were two best friends, a girl named Hope and a boy named Trusty.

Hope and Trusty were bright and curious. Like most children, they enjoyed exploring the world around them, and their curiosity often got them in trouble.

They lived in a large busy city with neat houses and shops, wide streets and beautiful buildings made of marble. Its people led comfortable lives. Their large fleet sailed the seas and brought back a variety of a variety of goods: from grain, wheat flour and salted fish, to exotic fabrics, incense and live animals, which were traded daily in a dusty noisy marketplace, called the Agora.

They worshipped twelve Gods who lived at the highest peak of Mount Olympus, a tall mountain always covered in clouds.

Their Gods enjoyed gifts and offerings of meat roasted over an open fire. The thick smoke that rose from the fire invited the Gods to their altars, where a share of the feast awaited them.

ne day, as Hope and Trusty were wandering around the Agora, they went past a pet store and noticed two beautiful pitch-black crows. They had long black legs, thick black bills and lustrous black feathers with a dark blue sheen. They were kept in a small cage and hopped restlessly from perch to perch.

As the friends approached to admire the birds, the two crows stopped and sat side by side on the highest perch. Each one elongated its neck and fixed an eye on Hope and Trusty, hoping these children might be the ones to free them from their cage.

"They are so beautiful. Look at their feathers!" said Hope, her eyes opening wide.

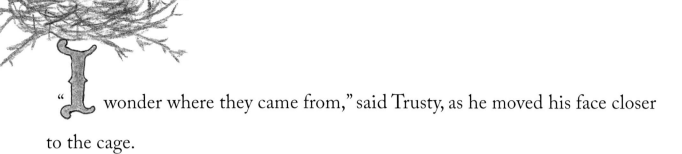

"I wonder where they came from," said Trusty, as he moved his face closer to the cage.

Kr-aack, kr-aack. "We came from the Land of the Birds," spoke one of the crows in a human voice.

Trusty jumped in surprise and Hope stepped back, tripped over Trusty's feet and fell over.

"This can't be real!" exclaimed Trusty as he helped Hope back to her feet. "No bird can speak with a human voice!"

Kr-aack, kr-aack. "Where we come from, all birds speak with a human voice. Our kingdom is magical," said the other crow, amused by the children's reaction. "Free us and we will take you there," he added with a strange twist in his voice.

At first, the two friends were bewildered. They looked at one another with raised eyebrows and moved away from the cage to talk it over, checking their little leather pouches and counting their pocket money. The crows hopped back and forth again in anticipation.

"I say we do it," said Trusty in a firm voice. "It is late summer and our friends have all gone to their country homes. Our parents are busy gathering grapes and it will be a couple of weeks before we join them in the countryside. Let's have some fun. Life in the city can be so boring in the summer."

Hope agreed to the plan without giving it much thought. They had just enough pocket money to purchase the birds and perhaps buy a few provisions for the journey.

Trusty was the one to break the news to the crows.

"We have decided to help you. But if we free you now, you'll fly away and we'll never see you again. Instead, we'll free you when we get there."

The crows thanked them for their kindness and promised them that they would not regret it. They warned Hope and Trusty that the journey would be a long one, so the two friends decided to return the next day better prepared for the trip.

The next morning, Trusty and Hope packed a flask of water, some bread, dried fruit and nuts. As soon as the marketplace opened, they rushed to the pet store. They bought the birds with the little pocket money they had and set forth to visit their kingdom.

The two crows guided Trusty and Hope with *kr-aacks* and *cawks* out of the city through the main gate. They followed a dirt road that led north, away from the cultivated fields and the summer estates of the city dwellers.

By midday, they had reached a noisy creek, where they sought temporary refuge under the maple trees that grew along its banks. A few nuts for the birds and some bread and dried fruit for the two friends was just what they needed before setting off again. The city was hardly visible in the distant horizon when the journey became mountainous, and the two friends began to get tired.

"Are we nearly there?" asked Hope, wiping the sweat from her forehead with the back of her hand.

"How much longer?" demanded Trusty, raising the cage to his face to communicate his urgency to the birds.

Kr-aack, kr-aack. "Not long," responded the crows. "We are almost there. The Land of the Birds lies beyond that hill. There, you will meet our king."

A winding trail led them up and over the hill. Just beyond the summit, they found themselves in a completely new world. A vast valley surrounded by mountain peaks lay before them. A bright green forest, streams and small lakes were visible on the horizon. And of course, there were thousands of birds flying everywhere, as far as the eye could see. Birds of all colors and sizes.

The two friends were frozen in awe, admiring this new world, when the sudden high-pitched cries of the crows startled them.

Cawk-cawk-cawk-cawk. Cawk-cawk-cawk-cawk, the two crows cried out as loud as they could, beating their wings excitedly in anticipation of freedom.

Drrrrrrrrrrr, cha-aa-ah, cha-aa-ah, replied a woodpecker from a nearby tree. "Who is calling for my king? What is your business with him?"

"We have come to meet your king," declared Trusty confidently.

"And see his kingdom," added Hope as she slowly opened the cage door to set the crows free.

The crows squeezed themselves out of the door and, in an act of gratitude, circled over Hope and Trusty's heads several times before landing, one on Hope's shoulder, the other on Trusty's. Hope and Trusty smiled and petted the birds' bellies with gentle strokes.

"Our king is taking his afternoon nap after dining on blueberries and locusts. I will wake him up if I must, but I warn you, he is not going to like this," the woodpecker said before disappearing behind a nearby thicket.

Oop, oop, oop, upupa, upupa! "Who dares disturb my sleep?" cried King Hoopoe as he flew from a bush. "What are you two doing in my kingdom? This is the Land of the Birds. Don't you know that humans are not allowed here?"

Trusty and Hope bowed their heads to King Hoopoe in respect, both taking a sneak peek at his colorful feathers.

"Your Highness, we have traveled far to visit your kingdom and we are very tired. With your permission, we would like to stay for a few days and admire your world before we return to our city," said Trusty respectfully.

The two crows joined in, *Kr-aack, kr-aack!* "Greetings, your Highness! These two humans helped us escape from the Land of the People. We promised them that they could explore our world in return. Could they stay with us for a while?"

The king shook his orange head with its tall, fanlike crest. "This is a serious matter. I cannot decide on my own." He turned to the woodpecker and said, "Wake up my wife, Queen Nightingale, and ask her to summon the birds with her divine singing. *They* will decide what to do with these two."

It wasn't long before the air was filled with the most beautiful melody human ears had ever heard! Trusty and Hope gasped in amazement as Queen Nightingale summoned the birds with enchanting notes and playful melodies.

A. ARVANITIS

Soon, King Hoopoe joined in with his own song. His summoning was heard at the four corners of the earth. It echoed across valleys, lakes and streams, over the tallest mountains and across the deep blue sea.

Oop, oop, oop, upupa, upupa. "My fellow feathered friends who feed in the sown fields, come forth."

Cheer-cheer-cheer, responded the robins. "We are on our way, Your Highness." And they let the worms live another day.

Oop, oop, oop, upupa, upupa. "My friends who bathe in the streams and fly over the tall mountains, come forth."

Kuk-kuk-kuk, replied the eagles. "We will be there, Our Lord." And they immediately abandoned the snake hunt.

Oop, oop, oop, upupa, upupa. "My friends who hunt insects in the marshes and chase the waves in the sea, come forth."

Chirp-chirp-chirp, answered the swallows. "We are coming, Our King." And they stopped chasing mosquitoes.

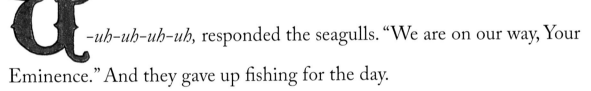

U*-uh-uh-uh-uh,* responded the seagulls. "We are on our way, Your Eminence." And they gave up fishing for the day.

O *op, oop, oop, upupa, upupa.* "And you who nest in the woodlands and the bushes, come closer. We have important issues to discuss."

Cheer-cheerie-cheer, responded the cardinals. "We are at your command, Your Highness." And they flew out of their hiding places.

Before long, the sky was filled with large and small flapping wings. Birds were pouring in from all over the world, abandoning the fields, the forests, the rivers, the sea, the mountains, and the cities, as they answered the call of their king.

Trusty and Hope watched with interest and amazement as birds of all sizes and colors began to line up in the trees around them.

awks, eagles and owls sat at the tallest branches. Then pigeons, sparrows, bluebirds, blue jays and swallows, robins and titmice, chickadees and cardinals took their places. Roosters, pheasants, peacocks, grouses and wild hens appeared through the bushes. The two crows perched on a nearby branch. They were all there, the ducks and the geese, the storks, the pelicans, and the seagulls. Even the swans and the flamingos flew from far away lakes, the parrots from distant lands, and the hummingbirds from the tropical forests. They all twittered with excitement and curiosity, eager to find out what this summoning was all about.

As Trusty and Hope took a good look around them, a sudden chill in their hearts made them search for one another's hand and hold it tight. Never before had they seen such a large gathering of birds! And they had reason to be scared. Not all birds were friendly…

Oop, oop, oop, upupa, upupa. The king's call echoed through the trees of the forest. "My feathered friends, we are all gathered here to decide whether these two humans, this boy Trusty and this girl Hope, should be allowed to stay with us in the Land of the Birds."

Gobble-gobble-gobble! "This is outrageous! We cannot allow humans here. They are our worst enemies," cried the wild turkey as he fluffed up his feathers and fanned his tail in anger.

Kr-aack, kr-aack, kr-aack. "They hunt us down for fun."

Quack-quack-quack. "They roast us in the oven with potatoes."

Chirp-chirp-chirp. "They kill us to make costumes and hats with our feathers."

Tweet-tweet-tweet. "They catch us with large nets and keep us trapped in zoos."

hooh, whooh, whooh. "They keep us in tiny cages in their houses, and expect us to sing for their amusement. Is that life fit for a bird? We will show no mercy to these humans."

Gobble-gobble-gobble! "Come! Birds of a feather flock together! Let's chase them out of our land with our pointed beaks."

The two friends drew even closer together and trembled in fear. They were about to turn around and run away when King Hoopoe addressed the bird assembly, "My friends, please hear me out. Trusty and Hope are kind children. They rescued two of our crows from the Land of the People and returned them home. Please give them a chance to speak for themselves."

As King Hoopoe and the two crows tried to hush the assembly, Trusty took a deep breath and stepped forward. His voice was heard loud and clear. He explained that neither he, nor his friend Hope, had ever harmed a bird in their lives. Instead, they admired birds for their flying and hunting abilities, their bright colors, their beautiful singing, and for their amazing elegance. "My feathered friends," called out Trusty in a steady voice, "I know that we humans have done you wrong, even though you deserve our respect. After all, you have been on this planet much longer than we and our twelve Olympian Gods have."

Hope stood behind him and nodded her head, looking shyly upward at the assembled birds through her long eyelashes.

The birds were now silent. Many tilted their heads to take a good look at the speaker. Others flew closer to better hear the boy. The truth and wisdom in Trusty's words caught their attention.

Encouraged by the birds' silence, Hope moved closer to her friend.

Trusty continued, "As we all know, at the beginning of time there was deep darkness and endless Night. Then, the dark feathered Night laid an egg. And out of it came the God of love, Eros, with sparkling golden feathers. Eros laid more eggs and created your race long before the earth, the sea, and the sky. Long before our Gods and we humans came into being."

The birds agreed with short cries, nodding at each other.

"Let me remind you, then, that back in the early days, you used to be kings and rulers of distant and prosperous lands," said Trusty, as he moved slowly through the assembly. "The rooster became the King of Persia, the cuckoo bird ruled over Egypt and Phoenicia, and the peacock used to be the King of India," continued Trusty, pointing at a colorful peacock in a nearby bush.

"Take a good look at him. He walks upright as a king. He still wears his tall, feathered crown and demonstrates his royal robe with pride. How many of you have not admired the jewels on his regal robe?"

"Yes! Yes! Very true. Very true," agreed the birds, looking at one another.

With sparkling eyes, Hope watched her friend win over the bird assembly. Seeing his success, she felt less scared and cautiously waited for a good time to jump in and participate.

Trusty continued, "Even our mighty God, Zeus, father of all Gods, has an eagle perching on his scepter. His wife, Hera, keeps a peacock as her favorite pet, and his daughter, the Goddess Athena, keeps an owl on her shoulder. Think of Hermes, the messenger of the Gods. He has a winged hat, holds a winged scepter and wears a pair of winged shoes."

Your words have brought us much sorrow and pain," interjected the wise old owl in a screeching voice.

"Our glorious past is too painful to remember," remarked Queen Nightingale. King Hoopoe nodded sadly.

"Very true. Very true," echoed throughout the forest, as the birds lowered their tails and heads in great disappointment.

"If only there was a way to restore our former glory and rise again," added an eagle from the tallest branch.

"Please, please, my feathered friends, do not despair," cried Hope to the assembly, finally grasping her chance to participate. She furrowed her brow, clasped her hands behind her back as she had seen her father do, and continued in a pensive tone, "Perhaps Trusty and I can help you become powerful again. I may have an idea."

"Go on!" added Trusty, looking at his friend with the utmost curiosity. Hope hesitated for a minute, but Trusty's commanding tone filled her with courage.

"First you need to do something daring and extraordinary. When the Gods and mankind take notice, seize the chance to place your demands and somehow make sure that they are fulfilled."

Questions erupted from all sides, as the birds demanded to know more.

Quack, quack, quack. "How can that be?"

Titu, titu, titu. "Explain yourself."

Cock a doodle-doooooo! "Tell us more!"

"What if you were to rule the skies by building your own city, high up in the clouds?" asked Hope with excitement, lifting her eyes up and raising both arms to the sky. "You could surround it with a tall, mighty wall and place guards at its doors. No one would enter without your permission. The Olympian Gods would have to share their power with you if they still wanted to receive their precious smoke from our offerings. And we humans would have to offer you treats and sweet delicacies with honey and nuts every time we sacrifice to our Gods, otherwise…"

"Otherwise, we will eat your crops, poop on your white marble buildings and let the mosquitoes bite you," interrupted the robin in a playful manner, winking at the assembly.

Outbreaks of laughter shook the forest. They laughed their hearts out, flapping their wings in excitement and wagging their tails like dogs.

Oop, oop, oop, upupa, upupa! "A city in the clouds!" exclaimed King Hoopoe, overwhelmed with joy. "Such a brilliant idea! Imagine! Our very own city in the clouds! It has never been attempted before. We will have to find an appropriate name for it…"

The birds began mumbling different names, Birdville… Bird Haven… Cloud-cuckoo-land… Cloudifornia… But somehow none of these names pleased the assembly, and eventually every head turned to the wise old owl in anticipation.

Finally, after a brief period of silence, the owl decided to share her wisdom. *Who-hoo-ho-oooooo.* "I believe I have the perfect name for our city." She pointed upward to the sky with a wing. "How about Ornithopolis, a bird city in the clouds?"

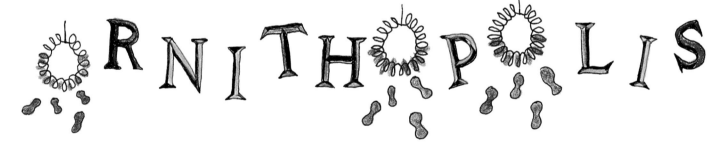

Oop, oop, oop, upupa, upupa! "That is a great name worthy of our bird city," declared King Hoopoe with excitement. "Ornithopolis it is! It is going to be a city like no other. We will all live together in peace and perfect harmony. The fellowship of birds will serve as an example to both Gods and humans alike."

"Come! Birds of a feather, work together!" ordered the king. "Fluff up your feathers, trim your beaks and sharpen your claws. We have a city to build. Choose the thickest cloud and let the work begin!"

Happiness overwhelmed the birds, large and small. Songs of joy filled the air. The assembly decreed that Hope and Trusty could stay in their land and help them build their city in the clouds. As an act of gratitude, they were presented with a magical root that made them grow temporary feathers, in likeness of their new friends.

Hope grew fluffy pink feathers around her body, like the flamingos, and Trusty grew pointed brown feathers along his arms, like the eagles.

While Hope and Trusty were busy admiring their feathers, King Hoopoe flew to the tallest branch and began directing the birds.

"We need thirty thousand cranes to fly to faraway lands in search of stones for our city-wall.

"And thousands of woodcocks, to break down the stones into square blocks.

"The storks will make mud bricks to build the walls of our city.

"And the ducks will have to fasten their aprons and lift the bricks high up in the clouds.

"The pelicans are going to bring water from the rivers and lakes and start making mud for our builders.

"Geese, get ready to shovel mud with your feet into deep nests made of branches and leaves.

"Eagles and hawks will grab the nests with their strong feet and bring them to the construction site.

"Hundreds of swallows will make sure that every builder has a trowel and does not run out of mud.

"And finally, woodpeckers, you are our carpenters. Sharpen your beaks and get ready to chop up wood and drill holes to make doors and windows."

When King Hoopoe finished assigning each bird a task, they began their work.

The cranes were the first ones to take off. They picked up their portable rafts and flew off to faraway lands to bring back stones. In the meantime, the woodcocks sharpened their beaks and prepared to chip away and shape the hardest of stones.

The pelicans flew to the banks of a nearby river and began mixing mud with their feet. Then the geese stepped in and shoveled it with their big feet into large nests provided by the eagles.

The storks set off to make sun dried bricks with the help of the pelicans, who carried water in large buckets. The ducks checked their aprons for holes and reinforced the stitches as they lined up and waited for the bricks to dry in the hot, blazing sun.

The woodpeckers set off to the forests and before long a familiar drilling sound filled the air as they brought down trees to make doors and windows for the buildings of their city.

In the days that followed all birds large and small, abandoned their lives on earth and united in perfect harmony to build their city in the clouds. Hope and Trusty did their best to help their new friends. Ornithopolis was a huge, noisy construction site, but before long a beautiful city rose above the clouds.
It was surrounded by tall walls with huge towers and strong gates.

Turkeys stood guard at the gates, making sure that no God or human entered the city without a valid traveling document. Hawks had offices next to the gates and were ready to stamp those documents with the official bird seal of entry. Seagulls flew swiftly from tower to tower, overseeing the procedure, ready to intervene if needed.

*U**pupa, upupa, oop, oop, oop!* "Our sky cloud city is finally complete! I am very proud of you, my friends. You may rest now and let the celebrations begin," proclaimed the king.

A thick white ribbon was placed at the main gate for the grand opening ceremony. As King Hoopoe lowered his crest and bent down to cut the ribbon with his beak, a messenger hummingbird darted out of nowhere. It hovered frantically in front of him, conveying a message of the utmost importance and greatest urgency.

There was an intruder among them! A Goddess had managed to sneak into the city through the gates, without presenting her papers to the turkeys at the main entrance.

It didn't take long before she made her presence known to King Hoopoe. It was the feathered Goddess Iris.

"What is the meaning of all this? Why have you blocked the skies?" demanded the Goddess. "The mighty Zeus, king of the Gods and ruler of mankind, sent me to find out why the people stopped making offerings to us. It has been over a week since we last received any smoke up on Mount Olympus and the Gods are becoming restless. In the name of Zeus, I order you to explain yourselves."

Oop, oop, upupa, upupa. "With all due respect, we don't need to explain ourselves, my fair Goddess," replied King Hoopoe, fluffing up his feathers and opening the fanlike crest to impress her. "From now on, we, the birds, are the rulers of the sky," he proclaimed with pride.

"You are no such thing!" shouted the Goddess, pointing her staff at him in anger. "Zeus will strike you down with his thunderbolt for this insolence."

Kuk-kuk-kuk! "All it takes is one word from Our King and we will fly to Mount Olympus and set your palaces ablaze," shrieked the eagles, showing no fear.

"No, my friends!" shouted King Hoopoe. "The fellowship of birds is wiser than that. Yes, we have the power to do so, but remember that with power comes great responsibility."

Turning to the Goddess, he added, "We are not looking for war, my fair Goddess. You may go back to Zeus and tell him that we will restore his communication with the humans. All we ask for in return is to be treated as equals and become co-rulers of the skies, like we used to be."

"You are a wise ruler, King Hoopoe. Your demands will be presented to Zeus without delay," agreed the Goddess in a softer tone. She spread her wings wide, getting ready to fly.

King Hoopoe asked a dove to escort the Goddess back to Mount Olympus,
carrying an olive tree branch as a peace offering to Zeus.

The little messenger was received with kindness and hospitality at Mount
Olympus. He was offered food and water, and was allowed a good rest before
facing the mighty Zeus, ruler of the Olympian Gods, god of the sky and bearer
of the thunderbolt.

Zeus was intrigued by this city in the skies. He could not help admiring the birds for their achievement. *If only humans could find a way to work and live together in harmony, like the birds have done, the world would be a better place,* he thought.

As he listened to the dove and Iris explain the birds' demands, Zeus stroked his beard and drew his eyebrows together. After a moment of silence that seemed like eternity to the little dove, he declared that the demands were reasonable. He decided to accept their peace offering with pleasure, and agreed to share the skies with them as equals.

A second dove was sent with an offering of goodwill to the people to negotiate terms with mankind. Their demands were to receive offerings of bird food and sweet delicacies every time humans gave sacrifices to their

Olympian Gods. In return, the birds would protect people's homes from rodents and snakes, their fields and crops from insects and worms. They would alert them to the change of seasons, show them when to plant their fields and when to prepare for winter. They would guide their ships to port safely, and warn them when bad weather was on the way.

The people had already suffered from the birds' absence, and were more than willing to accept the demands. Two weeks without birds meant clouds of insects eating their crops, thousands of worms destroying their fruit, hundreds of snakes living in their fields, countless mice raiding their homes, and numerous rats running up and down their streets.

In fact, people were so impressed by what the birds had achieved that not only did they agree to their terms, but they also began imitating their ways.

It was not long before they built mechanical wings to fly, and wrote music inspired by bird songs. They even paid tribute to the birds by naming their children after them. Doves became symbols of peace and everlasting love, hawks were venerated as Gods and eagles became the symbol of powerful empires.

As for Hope and Trusty, the two friends became honorary citizens of Ornithopolis. They built their own house at the city center, next to King Hoopoe's palace, and were free to come and go as they pleased.

In the years that followed, Trusty and Hope enjoyed many visits to Ornithopolis, bringing their friends and families to spend time in the skies with their bird friends.

But that was all long after the adventure that awaited them upon their arrival home…

Continue the Adventure with Hope & Trusty's Activity Books!

You and the young readers in your family or classroom can continue this excellent adventure with the delightful, interactive book that accompanies *Sky Cloud City*. Similar activity guides will be developed for upcoming books in *The Adventures of Hope & Trusty* series. In each activity book, kids will be engaged by drawings to color, cutouts, calligraphy to trace, puzzles, word searches related to the story and similar engaging activities.

Illustration Contest

Would your children like to become published illustrators? Encourage them to enter the ongoing illustration contest on our Sky Cloud City Facebook page, or by emailing hopeandtrusty@piercepress.com. The winner of the premiere Sky Cloud City contest is 10-year-old Andreas from Crete, Greece, who created the beguiling illustration in the front of this book.

The Series

All information related to this series can be accessed by scanning the QR code on this page or by visiting PiercePress.com. Books can be purchased at your local independent bookstore, on IndieBound.org, or at Amazon.com.

About the Author: *Maria Kamoulakou-Marangoudakis* was born in Athens, Greece, and spent her childhood steeped in the city's ancient art and architecture. From early on, Maria felt a strong calling to become an archaeologist, and went on to study archaeology in England in the late 1980s. She holds two degrees in the field, one with distinction. Maria's experience as a field archaeologist and a researcher with Greece's Hellenic Ministry of Culture spanned more than sixteen years. During that time, she worked in important archaeological sites throughout Greece, including Sparta, the Diros Caves, Patras, Aetolia-Akarnania, Epidaurus, the islands of Santorini, Lesvos, Zante and Kefalonia. Maria finished her career in Greece as a member of the 35th Ephorate of Prehistoric and Classical Antiquities in Kefalonia.

Following her marriage to Carl Marangoudakis, Maria moved to the United States in 2008. The seeds of her venture into children's literature were planted in 2012, during a stormy wintery night in New England. Maria had just emerged from a serious health adventure that left her with a strong desire to "seize the day" by reaching out to children. Using her background as a Greek archaeologist, Maria turned to her favorite ancient Greek playwright, Aristophanes, for inspiration. *The Adventures of Hope & Trusty: Sky Cloud City* is a free adaptation of the most fairytale-like of his comedies, *The Birds* (Ornithes). It is the first book in a series inspired by the most popular comedies of Aristophanes. You can find more information about the author at mariakamoulakou.com or at skycloudcity.com.

About the Illustrator: New England artist *Aspasia Tsihlakis Arvanitis* was born to a Greek-American family in Springfield, Massachusetts. From adolescence on, Aspasia had a strong inclination for painting and was attracted by the works of the Renaissance Masters. Her earliest training in oil painting took place during evening classes at Springfield Putnam High School in the early 1970s. She subsequently attended painting classes at the Museum of Fine Arts in Springfield and won a Humanities Award for Excellence in Fine Arts Painting at Springfield Technical Community College. She has taken private lessons in pastel and oil painting in Agawam, Massachusetts, and took a specialized course in Florida to learn the oil painting techniques of the Renaissance Masters. Aspasia enjoys experimenting with new techniques and styles in oil and pastel painting. Now in private collections in Europe and the United States, her compositions include portraits, landscapes, seascapes, still life, abstract and surrealistic paintings. Aspasia's favorite artistic subject matter is water reflection.